Dick Cate

BEN'S BIG DAY

Illustrated by Beryl Sanders

S I M O N & S C H U S T E R

LONDON • SYDNEY • NEW YORK • TOKYO • SINGAPORE • TORONTO

To Sue and Ken Stiles

Chapter One

Ben wasn't going to like his new school.

He knew that now, sure as eggs is eggs.

"How can you be so sure?" his mum called from the kitchen.

"Just am!" said Ben.

He flicked over channels on the telly: they were all boring.

"That Miss Kirby is horrible," he said. "She never smiles."

"Who says she never smiles?"

"Everybody. She makes you stand against walls."

"Who's everybody?"

"The boy from the paper-shop," said Ben.

"The boy from the paper-shop doesn't know everything," his mum said.

Ben noticed she didn't mention what the girl from upstairs had told her. She'd told his mum about a big rough boy at school whose name was Bernie Flowers. But his mum didn't mention that, of course.

She said, "You'll make a lot of new friends, just wait and see."

"I don't want new friends," he said.

"What *do* you want, Ben Adams?" his mum asked.

"I told you."

"No pets, Ben! We've already discussed that," she said.

He wasn't asking for anything fancy. Not a whole tribe of baboons. Not even one. Just a cat would do. If he had a cat he'd call it Bonzo.

"Fine name for a cat!" his dad always said.

Mrs Shastri, who lived on the ground floor of their house, had a cat called Santi. Whenever he came up to see them Ben's dad said, "Watch out, here comes Santi *Claws*!" because he dug his claws in really hard and sometimes bit you. But Ben didn't mind.

7

When they were in their other house Ben had almost talked his mum into having a cat. But just round the corner from Cable Street – where they lived now – there was a busy road. "No place at all to bring a cat up," his mum kept saying. "Besides, who'll be at home to look after it?"

That was because tomorrow she started her first job, answering the telephone at Broad Street Clinic, taking important messages. "I'm going to be a real somebody!" she kept saying. She was really excited, and dead nervous at the same time. She kept picking up their telephone at home and saying:

"Hello? Broad Street Clinic. How can I help you? Could you possibly come at six-thirty? Thank you for calling. Don't mention it."

She was just practising. There was nobody there. In fact, their phone wasn't even connected yet. "How am I doing?" she kept asking Ben. "Two out of ten," he kept saying back.

"Is there a little elf out there who could help me set this table?" she asked him now.

Ben didn't answer. He switched channels again. Still nothing on.

Which reminded him of something.

"It's not fair!" he shouted. "This school comes out too late for me to see the Rex Ritter cartoon on Tuesdays."

"Isn't that why your dad's getting us the video tonight, Ben Adams? And how can he afford the video if I don't go to work?"

Ben didn't answer. Sometimes it was no use arguing with grown-ups.

When his dad came home he called, "Sorry I'm late, woman. That meal smells like it's cooking itself real fine!"

"It *is* cooking itself real fine," said his mum. "Trouble is, this table in here could do with some help getting itself laid."

"Thought we had a boy in this house when I left?" said his dad.

"We did have," said his mum. "Only trouble is, that boy in there doesn't feel like helping. We need some handy elves in this house."

"Useful things to have about!" said Ben's dad as he came into the room. "How's tricks, Big Fry? Still looking forward to school?"

"No," said Ben.

"That's my boy!" said his dad.

"Miss Kirby never smiles," said Ben.

"Maybe she forgot to put her teeth in," said dad.

"There's a boy at this school who's really rough."

"RUFF! RUFF!" said his dad, pretending to be a dog.

"What should I do if he comes for me, Dad?"

"Float like a butterfly, and sting like a bee!" his dad said, coming for him, fists flying. He socked himself on the jaw, flew backwards through the air, and landed in a heap on the sofa.

He really was crazy, Ben's dad.

Chapter Two

"Hi, Ben!" said the Lollipop Lady next day as Ben crossed the busy road with his mum.

"Who's that?" Ben asked when they were safely over.

"Don't you remember? The lady in the church bazaar."

"Oh yeah," said Ben.

"You okay now, Ben?" his mum asked.

"No," said Ben. All he could see through the school railings was a lot of noisy kids. A big kid was buzzing round the yard with his arms stretched out, pretending to be an aeroplane. "I feel worse," he said.

"Like I say," his mum said, "I'll try and catch that half-past bus, but if I can't, remember to cross with the Lollipop Lady. You hear me, Ben? In you go now. I'll try my best to be here. Remember, Mrs Shastri's got our key. Give me a smile, honey, I have to scoot now. *Don't* swing that bag around, Ben. You could have an accident. You hear me?"

He watched her go. At the crossing she spoke to the Lollipop Lady. After she crossed the road she turned and waved. She looked worried. Ben tried to look worried too. He waved till a big lorry got in the way. The next time he could see across the road his mum had gone.

The first person he saw when he entered the yard was the boy from the paper-shop.

"Hi, kid!" said the paper-shop boy. "You okay?"

Ben nodded.

"If you need any help, just holler!" he said, and strolled off.

Ben felt better already.

He started swinging his Rex Ritter bag round his head.

"Hi, Ben! I like your Rex Ritter bag!"

It was the girl from upstairs. Her name started with an L and sounded like *train*, but he couldn't quite remember it. He pretended he hadn't noticed her and walked on.

Wrrrummm! Wrrrummm! went the bag as he swung it round his head. *Wrrrummm-wrrrummm!* When Rex Ritter swung his bag around his head it whirled him off to somewhere safer. Ben wouldn't have minded that now. He swung the bag round his head even faster. *Wrrrrrummmmm-wrrrrrummmmm!*

Then: WOMP!

"What did you do that for?"

It was the big kid he'd seen buzzing round the yard a minute ago – The Human Aeroplane – and he was glaring down at him.

The side of his face was red where Ben's bag had hit him.

Chapter
Three

Back and back he pushed Ben. He used just one finger. It didn't hurt. But Ben didn't like it.

The girl from upstairs was watching them. She looked scared.

The boy from the paper-shop saw what was happening, but he looked the other way. Maybe *he* was scared as well.

Ben had his back against the wall now. There was only one thing to do. He remembered what his dad had said; but it's hard floating like a butterfly when a big boy is poking you, and even harder stinging like a bee. Every time he hit out the big boy just laughed.

"What on earth is going on here?" said a sharp voice. It was a strict teacher. She wasn't smiling, and Ben was pretty sure she was Miss Kirby. "Are you bullying?" she asked the big boy.

"No, miss," he said.

"What's your name?"

"Bernie Flowers, miss."

"I've heard of you," she said. "Were you bullying this boy?"

"No, miss. He hit me first."

"Oh, yes? Did you hit this big boy first?" she asked Ben.

"Yes," said Ben.

"Pardon?" she said. "You don't have to be scared of this boy. Tell me the truth."

Ben said nothing.

"Are you absolutely sure you hit him first?" she asked.

Ben nodded.

"In that case you can *both* stand against this wall," she said. "You here, Bernie Flowers, and you over here, little boy. And no talking!"

"That was Miss Kirby," said Bernie Flowers as she stalked away. "She's new and can't help it. What's your name, kid? You saved my life."

Ben told him.

"Mine's Bernie Flowers," said Bernie Flowers.

Ben didn't say anything.
Bernie held his hand out,
flat. "Slap my hand,
kid," he said.
"What for?"
"Never mind what for,
just slap it."
Ben slapped his hand.
"Right on!" said Bernie.
"Now hold your hand out."
Ben held his hand out
and Bernie slapped it.
"Now we're pals for life!"
said Bernie, grinning.

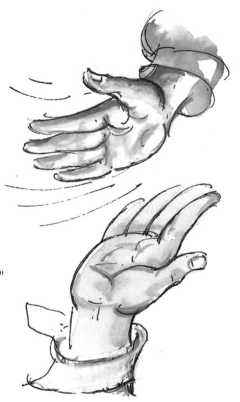

"I saw that!" shouted Miss Kirby, coming back.
"Bullying again!"

"I wasn't, miss," said Bernie. "We were just making
pals. Honest."

"For life," said Ben, smiling up at her.

"Are you sure?" said Miss Kirby.

And she almost smiled back at them.

Chapter Four

When Miss Kirby introduced him to the class everybody clapped, and a boy with big ears shouted out: "HIP-HIP-HOORAY!"

Ben tried to stay cool.

"Does anybody know Ben already?" asked Miss Kirby.

"I do, miss," said the girl from upstairs.

"Then perhaps he could sit at your table, Lorraine," said Miss Kirby.

That was her name! Ben remembered it now.

After that they did hard
sums. Ben had a lot of
rubbings-out. Lorraine
lent him her pencil-case
which had a rubber in it
and a pencil-sharpener.
You went up for marks
when you'd done five,
and Ben got five crosses.

He knew he'd been right about this school now, sure
as eggs is eggs.

He spent the rest of the lesson sharpening his pencil.

At playtime Miss Kirby made Bernie stay at one end
of the yard and Ben at the other. Every time she wasn't
watching Bernie stuck both thumbs up and winked.
Ben wasn't sure what it meant, but he kept doing it
back.

After break, when they were all sitting quietly, a
man teacher carried in a heavy parcel-thing covered
in brown paper and plonked it on a table.

"Thank you so much, Mr Salter," Miss Kirby said.
"Very kind."

"Don't mention it, Miss Kirby," Mr Salter said as he
went out. "It's a weight off my mind!"

"Is it Mrs Brown's aquarium, miss?" asked a girl with
red hair.

"Quite right, Felicity," said Miss Kirby. "And what do
you think is in it?"

"A fish, miss?" said Felicity Red-hair.

"Good guess, Felicity, but not quite right."

"SHARKS!" shouted the boy with big ears. "JAWS! I seen it on telly!"

"If we're going to be silly, Charles, it goes back where it came from!"

"Is it a pet, miss?" asked Lorraine.

"Well done, Lorraine!"

"Thought you didn't like pets, miss?" said Felicity.

"Normally I don't," said Miss Kirby, "but Mr Salter suggested it."

"Is it a hamster, miss?"

"Bigger than a hamster."

"ORANG-UTANG!" shouted Charles, his ears sticking out like small paddles.

"I shan't speak again, Charles!"

"I hope it's not a rat, miss," said Felicity. "I hate rats!"

"It isn't a rat."

"Let's have a look, miss!"

Miss Kirby removed the brown paper and they all saw eyes like almonds, a long tail made entirely of skin, and long twitchy whiskers.

"It *is* a rat, miss!" said Felicity. "Look at its tail and whiskers!"

"It's not a rat, Felicity. It's a gerbil!"

"It's horrible, miss!"

"Lift it out, miss," said somebody.

"All right. If you want me to."

Miss Kirby didn't seem too keen, but she removed the wire-netting top and lifted the gerbil out. She put it on her other hand, so they could all see it.

Everybody flooded round, shouting, and then an awful thing happened.

The gerbil shifted, it was hard to see what happened, "*Ow!*" said Miss Kirby, "*Oooh!*" and jerked her hand, and the gerbil fell on the floor: PLOP!

Chapter Five

"OOOOOH!" they all shouted, and flooded back, all except one boy.

Ben didn't move. Neither did the gerbil. They both stayed perfectly still.

"I wonder if somebody would care to pick it up?" said Miss Kirby.

"NO WAY!" said Charles.

"Why don't you, miss?" asked Felicity.

Miss Kirby didn't say anything. She looked down at her finger.

"Have I to go for Mr Salter, miss?" asked Felicity.

That was when Ben bent down and picked up the gerbil. Its heart was beating fast. He held his hand over the aquarium so that if it fell again it wouldn't hurt itself this time, but made his hand flat so everybody could see it. Its whiskers started twitching again and it looked at him.

People flooded closer.

"It might easy bite again!" said Charles.

"He's only small," said another boy.

"Small animals sometimes have MONSTER teeth!" said Charles.

Ben said nothing. He wasn't scared at all.

"Would you like to lower him back down now, Ben?"
said Miss Kirby. "That's fine." She put the wire-netting
lid back on and made sure it was safe.

"I can see you're a brave boy, Ben," she said, looking
down at him. "Maybe I was wrong about this morning.
Maybe that big boy wasn't bullying you at all?"

"He wasn't, miss," said Ben.

"I like a brave boy, Ben," she said, "and an honest
boy as well." And she definitely smiled this time.
"Now if everybody will sit in their places I'd like you to
draw our gerbil while I write some notes on the board."

Chapter Six

"Hi, Ben!" This time it was one of the dinner ladies, the one in charge of chips. "Wonder how your mum is getting on?"

"He's shy," said Lorraine who happened to be just behind him in the queue.

"I expect his mum is shy by now as well," said the dinner lady. "All that answering the telephone!" She put her chip-scoop to her ear and pretended it was a telephone. *"Hilloo? Hilloo? Who's your lady-friend?"*

All the other dinner ladies laughed.

"I expect you'll be setting out the table for your mum tonight before she comes home, won't you, Ben?" said the chip lady. "She'll be worn to a shadow – like all us girls!"

All the dinner ladies laughed again. They didn't look like shadows to Ben.

They were still laughing when Bernie came and sat down beside him. He had a mountain of chips and poured half a bottle of ketchup over them. Then he made a face at Lorraine.

"She's okay," said Ben. "She lent me her pencil-case this morning."

"Sorry, Pencil-case," Bernie said to her. "I never knew that."

"How come you got so many chips?" said Ben.

"The chip lady's my mum's best friend," said Bernie. "You want half?"

"No thanks," said Ben.

Bernie gave him half anyway. He asked Lorraine if she wanted some but she went pink and shook her head and that seemed to start Bernie grunting.

Felicity Red-hair put up her hand and said,
"Please Mr Salter, Bernie Flower's making his
animal noises again."

"Wonders never cease!" said Mr Salter, coming
over.

"He's not supposed to do it in the dining-hall, sir,"
said Felicity.

"I should think not," said Mr Salter. "The farmyard
would be a more appropriate place. Or the zoo.
Were you making animal noises, Bernie?"

Bernie grunted.

"That seems perfectly clear," said Mr Salter. "In
that case —"

"He won't do it again, sir," said Ben.

"Who are you?" asked Mr Salter. "The official animal trainer round here?"

"We're pals, sir," said Ben.

"Pals? With this boy here?" said Mr Salter. "With Bernie Flowers?"

"You won't grunt again, will you, Bernie?" said Ben.

Bernie shook his head.

"You're sure you can stop yourself, Bernie?" asked Mr Salter.

"No sweat!" said Bernie, and stuffed seventeen chips in his mouth.

Chapter Seven

When Ben came out of school at hometime Bernie was waiting for him. As they walked together past the school railings Ben saw an amazing thing: Miss Kirby crossing the yard with Mr Salter, and smiling all over her face.

Ben didn't say anything to Bernie because he was talking about a gas mask his uncle had found from the war.

"Shame, Ben," said the Lollipop Lady as they crossed the busy road, "looks like your mum didn't make the half-past bus after all. You go straight home now."

"It's okay, Mrs Bride," said Bernie Flowers. "I'm looking after him now."

"That'll be nice for him, Bernie," said Mrs Bride. "I'll tell your mum you're being useful for a change and she'll be real pleased."

They were just looking at some gorilla masks in the paper-shop window when Lorraine passed them, pretending to look the other way.

"Hi, Pencil-case!"
said Bernie.

"Her real name's
Lorraine," explained Ben.

"Hi, Lorraine Pencil-
case!" said Bernie.

Lorraine went pink,
but sort-of smiled.

Then they started looking at the gorilla masks
again.

"I'd really like one of those," said Bernie.

"You don't really need one, Bernie!" said Ben. "You
look like a gorilla already!"

Bernie laughed. He had teeth like Santi, only
bigger.

When they reached Ben's street Bernie said, "See
you tomorrow. I'll come round for you straight after
tea. Show you where this canal is I know about. My
uncle says it goes all the way to China."

"Where is it?" said Ben.

Bernie waved his hand vaguely in the air. He
knocked against Mrs Shastri's tree and some of its

white petals fell on the pavement. Mrs Shastri wouldn't like that. Ben looked at her windows but she wasn't watching.

"So see you later, alligator!" said Bernie.

"In a while, crocodile!" said Ben.

"Ben, I want to ask you a big favour," said Mrs Shastri when he called for the key. "Next week we're going to Birmingham to see Mr Shastri's brother. Could you look after Santi for us, for the weekend?"

"I'd like that, Mrs Shastri," said Ben. "I'd really like that."

"You ask your mum, okay?"

"I will."

"You want me to come up with you, Ben?" she asked.

Ben shook his head and hurried upstairs. He had a lot of important things to do before his mum got home.

First he stuck his picture to the wall where everybody would see it. His gerbil seemed to be floating in the air and he'd had to stick an extra bit on its tail because the first time he'd missed. But Miss Kirby had said nobody was perfect and given him an extra big tick.

Then he went into the kitchen and set the table properly. After that he did his homework while he demolished a packet of his dad's favourite biscuits – the ones he called Suggestives. Then he lay back on the sofa with a cushion behind his head, trying to look real cool.

When his mum came home she said, "Sorry I couldn't pick you up, honey, but it won't happen again. How was school?"

"Fine," said Ben. "How was work?"

"They're talking about putting me in charge already!" said his mum.

"By the way," said Ben, "Mrs Shastri wants us to look after Santi at the weekend. I told her I would do it. Okay?"

"That'll be nice for you," she said. "You're sure you can manage?" Then she must have seen his picture because she shrieked and said, "My goodness! Who did this fabulous drawing?"

"It's nothing," he said.

"Nothing?" she said. "It's lovely. What is it? A kangaroo?"

"A gerbil," said Ben. "We have one at school."

"And what's this squiggle at the bottom?"

"Its baby," said Ben

"Has it got a baby as well?"

"Miss Kirby said we have to use our imaginations," said Ben.

"Well I think that's lovely! Anything else happen at school?"

"Nothing," said Ben.

When she went in the kitchen she shrieked again.

39

"Who's set this table? That you, Ben Adams?"

"Must've been the good little elves!" he said.

"I do like a few good little elves about the house!" his mother said.

When his dad came home he said, "How were things, Big Fry?"

"Awful," said Ben. "We had to work. I got five crosses in a row."

"Success at last!" said his dad. When he saw the picture he staggered back and said, "Who stuck this kangaroo thing up on our wall?"

"It's a gerbil," said Ben.

"If it's a gerbil, why is it springing through the air?"

"It's a springy gerbil," said Ben. "The floor was springy as well."

"What's this squiggly bit down the bottom?" asked his dad.

"That's its baby," said Ben.

"You could've fooled me," said his dad. "I thought it was something else!"

"Never mind that," said Ben's mum. "You see that big tick?"

"It's a real big tick, and the kangaroo's real springy," said his dad.

"Come in this kitchen and give me a real big hug and kiss!"

"That I can do," said Ben's dad, going in. "You survived, then, woman?"

"Just about. Now put me down and give me a hand with these vegetables."

"Vegetables? How many times I have to tell you, woman? I know nothing about vegetables. I haven't even learnt how to catch them yet!"

"I'll catch them, you skin them," Ben's mum said. "You can start on that cauliflower."

"This here thing a cauliflower?" asked Ben's dad. "Or is this what they calling a melon nowadays? And why are all the spoons on this table inside-out and the forks upside-down?"

"The good little elves must have been," said Ben's mum.

"They must've been real mixed-up little elves!" said Ben's dad, "Not to mention they've been at my favourite Suggestive biscuits!"

Chapter Eight

They were almost finished eating when there was a knock at the door.

Ben's mum went to answer it.

"You've got a visitor, Ben!" she called. "It's Lorraine. Say hello," she said as she brought her in.

"Hello," said Ben, keeping his mouth stiff, "Lorraine."

"Real friendly!" said his dad. "When you two getting married?"

"I heard Ben tell Miss Kirby his favourite programme was Rex Ritter so I brought round my video of *The Complete Adventures*," said Lorraine.

Ben felt a smile growing inside him. He had felt it growing all day, but now it was getting really big.

"Ben *talked* to Miss Kirby?" said his mum.

"With his own mouth?" said his dad.

Lorraine nodded. "He was very brave, Mrs Adams. Miss Kirby dropped the gerbil and Ben picked it up. And Bernie Flowers has hardly knocked anybody over today because Ben has sort-of tamed him. Almost."

"You didn't tell me that, Ben," said his mum.

"I forgot."

"How did you do it, son?" asked his dad.

"I floated like a bee, Dad, and stung him like a butterfly."

"That's my boy!" said his dad.

"Miss Kirby gave us some homework," said
Lorraine. "We have to think of a name for our gerbil.
You done yours yet, Ben?"

Ben nodded.

"What you going to call him, son?" asked his dad.

"Bonzo," said Ben.

"Fine name for a kangaroo," said his dad.

The video man called soon after that and the
others watched him fix it up while Ben finished his
third helping of ice-cream.

He smiled to himself as he ate. Pretty soon he'd be
watching *The Complete Adventures*, and tomorrow
he'd have two pals at school. Two was all you
needed, really. Though he might make friends with
the boy called Charles. He liked boys with sticking-
out ears.

He started clearing the table, doing it quietly so his mum wouldn't hear a sound.

It would be great having Bernie Flowers as a friend. Like having a baboon, really. A whole tribe of them.

And he remembered Miss Kirby smiling all over her face as she crossed the yard and he wondered if he was somehow responsible.

"You coming in, Superman?" his dad called.

Ben placed the last plate on the side, quietly, so that no-one would hear. Then he went in, trying to look real cool but feeling pretty good inside because he knew he was going to like his new school.

He knew that now.

Sure as eggs is eggs.

Ben knows he won't like his new school.
He's been told his teacher is grumpy, and
there's a big rough boy in his class.
But, on his very first day, Ben makes friends
with the big boy *and* he makes Miss Kirby smile.
Perhaps school won't be so bad after all . . .

This funny, warm story about Ben's big day at
his new school is perfect for reading alone.

UK£2.99
ISBN 0-7500-0262-X

299

SIMON & SCHUSTER
YOUNG BOOKS

9 780750 002622